# Andrea Zimmerman & David Clemesha

# Fire Engine Man

**Henry Holt and Company**
**New York**

Henry Holt and Company, LLC
Publishers since 1866
175 Fifth Avenue
New York, New York 10010
mackids.com

Library of Congress Cataloging-in-Publication Data
Zimmerman, Andrea Griffing.
Fire engine man / Andrea Zimmerman and David Clemesha.—1st ed.
p.      cm.
Summary: A young boy imagines the work he will do and the safety gear he will wear when he
becomes a fireman some day, as his younger brother first watches then joins him on the job.
ISBN 978-0-8050-7905-0
[1. Firefighters—Fiction.  2. Brothers—Fiction.  3. Imagination—Fiction.]  I. Clemesha, David.  II. Title.
PZ7.Z618Fhr 2007      [E]—dc22      2006007909
First Edition—2007
Printed in China by RR Donnelley Asia Printing Solutions Ltd., Dongguan City, Guangdong Province

10

The artists used acrylic on Bristol paper to create the illustrations for this book.

**For Amber and Hunter**

# I love fire engines.

I like to squirt down fires.

# I'm going to be a fire engine man.

I will wear a special coat and boots and a hat to protect me.

I will drive my own big fire engine.

It will have a loud siren and flashing lights.

My brother can see me pass by.

I will hook up my hose.

I will help the other firefighters fight the fire.

When the fire is out, I will drive back to the station.

At the fire station, I will have more work to do.

My brother could visit me there,
because it would be safe.

He could sit in the fire engine.

I could make a snack for us in the fire station kitchen.

He could see my bunk and maybe even take a nap.

# But if the alarm rang,
# I would have to go.

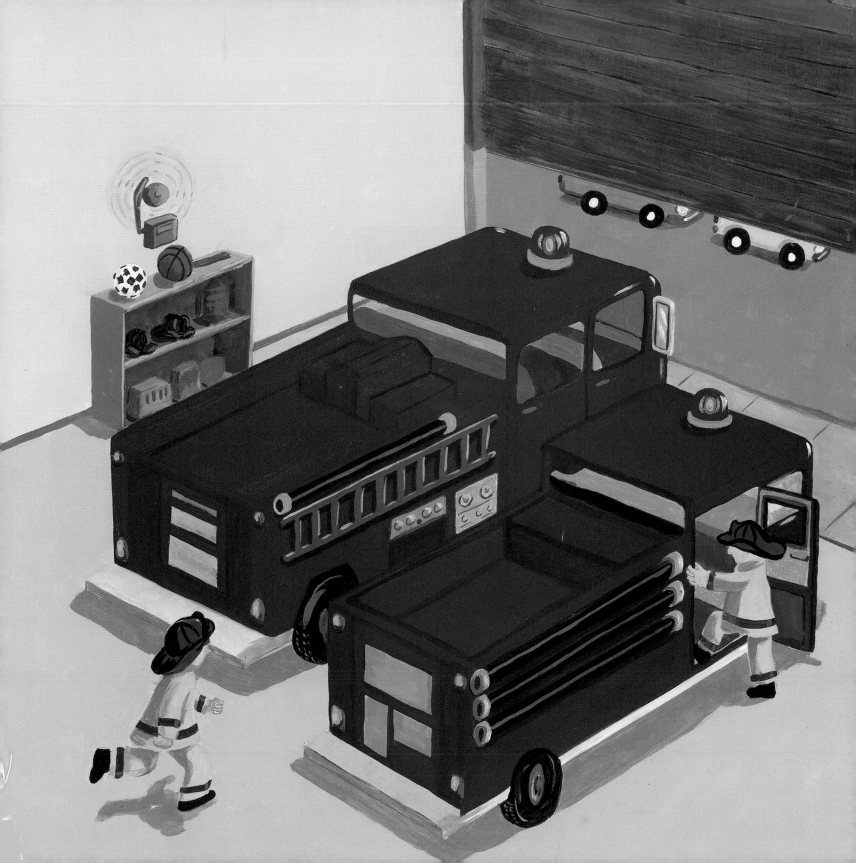

I will always be ready.

I will drive my fire engine.

I will squirt down all the fires
when I am a fire engine man.

He can be a fire engine man, too.

When my brother gets bigger, he can help.